CW00602183

Curaçao

Curaçao

A Cat and her Friends

Agneta Näslund

SOUVENIR PRESS

To my three cats,
Lisa Curaçao,
Cassis and Seagram

First published in Sweden by
Bokförlaget Trevi, Stockholm,
under the title *Katt efter Katt*

First British edition published 1993 by
Souvenir Press Ltd, 43 Great Russell Street,
London WC1B 3PA

ISBN 0 285 63164 0

Photoset by Rowland Phototypesetting Ltd,
Bury St Edmunds, Suffolk

Printed in Italy by
New Interlitho, Trezzano

W hy do I take pictures of cats?

Because I enjoy photography and because cats are so exceedingly beautiful. In fact it all started as a game, but soon it developed into a challenge—to get as close as possible, not only physically, but mentally as well; to try to capture the qualities I respect most in cats: their joy of living, their pride, their complete serenity.

My cats have never been 'just' animals. They have become my closest friends.

Curaçao was called Lisa at first. It was only later we settled for Curaçao which is a play on words. I was lying on my bed talking to her, and I heard her purring and told her that her purring sounded just like 'curaçao'.

Crème de Cassis is a liqueur made from blackcurrants, and I thought that the colour of blackcurrants resembled that of my black friend.

Seagram was a little more difficult. For some strange reason the two other cats had been named after different alcoholic drinks, so I started trying to think of another one. Since Seagram's coat is partly the colour of whisky, especially on his tummy, he was given the name of my favourite brand of whisky, Seagram. He has never answered to that name.

All three cats are of mixed breed—domestic shorthair with a touch of Siamese or . . . it's not easy to tell. I do know, however, that all three have totally different personalities.

Curaçao was my first cat. I shall never forget the spring day when I went to fetch her. A soft grey, sleepy, warm little body was put into my hands. She was the most beautiful creature I had ever seen, and suddenly I realised that she was to be *my* responsibility, and mine alone. Would I be able to manage? What were we going to learn about each other? The picture showing her lying asleep on her back on a white sheet was one I took that very first day.

Curaçao is the cat I have photographed most, and one of the reasons for this is technical: she is grey. (Cassis is so black that he is almost impossible to photograph.) But naturally I was also so charmed by her that I wanted to share every moment of her life. Her first fly, the first time she succeeded in jumping onto the window-sill, the first time she opened the wardrobe door. The white cat she is sleeping beside in one of the pictures is called Sluggo and was a boarder in our house for a few weeks.

Cassis, the black one, is the most 'difficult' of the three cats. When he was young he wore his nerves on the outside. Imagine how happy I was when I noticed that he was beginning to trust me more and more. With age and trust his nervousness has mellowed to a kind of sensibility. He and I have deep conversations with each other—with me lying on the couch and Cassis on my chest gazing straight into my eyes. These conversations are wordless but very intense. When Cassis was a kitten Curaçao was rather unkind to him, so he has always felt a little inferior and he gets depressed easily.

Tigerstriped Seagram is the youngest. He takes what he wants from life. He is a plucky cat and confidently assumes that everyone he meets will love him. When Cassis and I have our conversations he comes up to us, very jealous, and breaks up our tête-à-tête: 'Hey, *I'm* here now!' In a very superior way he makes it plain that nothing is impossible, especially for him! If he sees that Cassis is unable to jump onto the refrigerator he dashes forward and launches himself into the air, and when he is sitting on top of the refrigerator he turns round and looks down on Cassis, and I am sure he says, 'Piece of cake, my boy!' His favourite place is up there, preferably on top of all the toilet rolls we keep there, high up under the ceiling.

Our whole apartment and the way it looks have been designed and planned for and by the cats. A 'tasty' flower is for eating, a poisonous flower must be thrown out. Visitors are fascinated by a small Bokhara rug on the desk chair (placed there for Seagram who likes a soft bed), the half-open bathroom door (their litter tray is in there and the door must never be closed) and the rubber bands on the window-catches to stop people opening the windows wide (the cats cannot be allowed to take a walk outside).

Visitors who do not own cats look very surprised when I take out a small foot-stool and put it on the kitchen bench, so that Cassis will be able to jump up on the refrigerator without falling off. Normal behaviour is not to be expected, nor does the apartment look as pristine as it did before the cats moved in.

Like so many other cat-owners I sometimes buy a new toy for my cats. To make the cats happy? Hardly. They prefer other, more sophisticated toys that can stimulate their imagination—simple things like a piece of paper rolled into a ball, or freshly cooked spaghetti, for instance. Seagram's favourite plaything is a green ribbon with two knots in it. He asks me to throw it for him, and then he springs up and catches it in mid-air, grabbing it between his paws. Then he takes it in his mouth and lays it in front of the person whom he wants to throw it again. Cassis fetches things too, but his favourite is a small plastic ring. Curaçao has a small piece of fur which, in her view, is highly dangerous and she has to kill it over and over again. But, strange as it may seem, it never dies completely. In the photographs you can see her turning somersaults and attacking something woolly and savage.

Sometimes they lie in ambush. When Cassis goes to the loo Seagram sits behind the bathroom door waiting and waiting . . . Cassis pokes his head out very cautiously to see if the coast is clear, and then Seagram throws himself on Cassis in a huge leap. It never fails—they are both frightened out of their wits.

They certainly have imagination. They also have integrity and pride. These qualities, among others, are why I think so highly of cats. The cat is its own master and goes its own way.

Agneta Näslund

Now, from the dark, a deeper dark,
The cat slides,
Furtive and aware,
His eyes still shine with meteor spark
The cold dew weights his hair.
Suspicious,
Hesitant, he comes
Stepping morosely from the night,
Held but repelled,
Repelled but held,
By lamp and firelight.

Now call your blandest,
Offer up
The sacrifice of meat,
And snare the wandering soul with greeds,
Give him to drink and eat,
And he shall walk fastidiously
Into the trap of old
On feet that still smell delicately
Of withered ferns and mould.

ELIZABETH COATSWORTH

Cats have an admirable completeness, a sensory ability that we may never fully know or understand: but even so, it is hard for us to tell how aware they are of their own individuality. Do they have a sense of who and what they are? Some would argue that this is impossible, but having rigid opinions about cats' psychology can lead to a very narrow view of them, one which we are already having to alter in the light of new experience.

Although much has been written on modifying your cat's behaviour by the way you treat it, and tests have shown that the theories work successfully in practice, little is known (except by cat owners) of how a cat's behaviour is affected by the more subtle signals it receives through being 'in sympathy' with its owner's feelings.

You react without being aware of it to your cat's moods. A depressed cat makes your spirits sink, a happy cat makes you feel good. The reason for this may be that if your cat is happy it reassures you that you are taking care of it both physically and emotionally. Equally, if the cat is depressed you will feel that you have somehow been neglectful in your relationship with it: you may worry that it might be unwell. Conversely, people who are close to their cats say that their pets are able to detect their moods. Perhaps their happiness reassures the cat that everything is fine, just as their bad moods make the cat feel more anxious.

Either way, the consequences are the same: if you are happy, the chances are that your cat will feel happy; if you are depressed or irritable, your cat may also feel upset. Either of you may influence the other's state of mind.

The basic independent nature of cats seems to save most of them from being overtly reactive to our feelings; dogs do not have this protection and are more susceptible to the influence of instinctive sympathy. This is perhaps because dogs, as pack animals, are by nature more alert to our moods; conforming to the commands of the leader is very important to them. If the leader is displeased they may get a nasty bite—it's enough to make anyone more susceptive!

A kitten born in the wild may never fully respond to people. It will accept your food and the comfort of your home, but it may never lose its natural self-preservation instinct which makes it nervous and wary of people. Such a cat, along with those which have had insecure kitten-hoods, or have experienced a traumatic event in their lives, or who simply have a nervous personality, are most likely to be sensitive to others' anxieties, as they see and feel all of life as threatening. They are more adept at picking up others' stresses since a stressful animal or human is a potential danger to them.

A cat which has had a secure kittenhood and a reasonably happy life is more likely to be self-confident and so less affected by the emotions of others. This is not to say that such cats are insensitive to our negative feelings. The confidence they have acquired through being exposed to people from an early age, and always feeling safe and contented, will tend to make them more responsive to our moods but less disturbed by our negative emotions.

Although we domesticate cats, they still live part of their lives as wild cats. But if you establish a close relationship with your cat by giving it your time and attention, it will be more likely to respond to you. Each of you will project onto the other and your lives will become entangled as you develop a sensitivity to one another's moods. Certainly a number of pedigree breeds, including Siamese and Burmese cats, enjoy the company of their human companions and have a keen ability to sense and react to our feelings. They also display a higher level of intelligence than the average cat: perhaps a history of close contact with human beings who have lavished attention on them has released more of their potential.

Cats may become withdrawn if they feel insecure and frightened, and may lead their own lives more intensely. The extent to which a cat can walk alone and deal with its anxiety in its own undramatic way does mean that problems of this nature are much more likely to be overlooked in cats than in dogs. If your neurotic dog starts snarling at—or biting—visitors, you should clearly take some action. If your neurotic cat withdraws into itself and walks alone, the problem can mount up over a long period without your being aware of it. The cat's tendency to aloofness, and its basic independence, are mirrors and symbols of the unconscious—something hidden and unseen which you can never fully know or control.

VIVIENNE ANGUS

Cats will watch creatures, activities, actions unfamiliar to them, for hours. The making of a bed, the sweeping of a floor, packing or unpacking a case, sewing, knitting—anything, they will watch. But what are they seeing? A couple of weeks ago, black cat and a couple of kittens sat in the middle of the floor and watched me cut cloth. They observed the moving scissors, the way my hands moved, the way the cloth was put in different heaps. They were there, absorbed, all morning. But I don't suppose they were seeing what we think. What, for instance, does grey cat see when she watches, for half an hour at a time, the way motes move in a column of sunlight? Or when she looks at the leaves moving in the tree outside the window? Or when she lifts her eyes to the moon over the chimney pots?

Black puss, meticulous educator of her kittens, never loses an opportunity for a lesson or a moral. Why should she spend a morning, a kitten on either side, watching the flash of metal in dark cloth, why does she sniff the scissors, sniff the cloth, walk around the field of operations and then communicate some observation to the kittens, so that they perform the same actions—interspersed, since they are kittens, with all kinds of tricks and games? But they sniff the scissors, sniff the cloth, do what their mother has just done. Then sit and watch. She is learning something and teaching them, there is no doubt of it.

Doris Lessing

Contrary to expert advice, Minna wears a collar—an elegant green collar with an identity disc and two brass bells. A collar, I have heard, is undesirable because it may catch in the spikes of railings or the branches of a tree, but in my experience this risk is negligible if a cat is trained to a collar when very young. It is possible that a grown cat may so resent the introduction of a collar that he will try to drag it off and thereby injure himself but I have never heard of an instance.

Minna is proud of her collar and plainly enjoys wearing it. She puts the bells to practical use, whenever she wants to be admitted to a room, by shaking her head outside the closed door. She does not worry if she is late for breakfast, knowing that the tinkle of her bell will cause the door to be opened. Sometimes when she rings outside the door I delay, for the satisfaction of hearing her tinkle imperiously repeated. And with what an air of affronted majesty she stalks into the room if she has been thus kept waiting! Custom brings her to the dining-room at breakfast time, not hunger, for as often as not she turns up her aristocratic nose at the fish or milk offered her.

Minna has also learned to summon her kittens by sounding her bells. When the babies get to the exploring stage and escape from the maternal eye in house or garden Minna recalls them by an agitated peal. They usually answer the summons promptly but Minna will continue to ring until they do.

Minna can silence her bell as effectively as she can ring it. Not a sound is to be heard when she stalks a bird. What a waste of time it is to 'bell the cat' with the intention of suppressing natural instincts!

Michael Joseph

How well cats understand sounds that come to them from our gadget-filled world is difficult to interpret, much less how they might be able to use them to their own advantage. I know a woman named Christine who has a cat with one of the strangest behavioural patterns I have encountered this side of the edge of reality. She installed a television set in her bedroom, the kind with the push-pull buttons for ON and OFF. Simply, there is a little plastic button on the control panel beside the screen and when it is pulled out you have television. One morning at five-thirty (!), shortly after she installed the box, she was awakened by the terribly disturbing sound of someone counting, very loudly. It was an early morning exercise show, a hideous assault on a sensitive mind. She was alone in her apartment with her cat, who was now sitting on top of the television console looking smug.

'All right,' she said, once the panic had subsided and she was some-what in control, 'I might as well feed you.'

It was a fatal error. She reinforced her cat's behaviour by rewarding him for committing a dastardly act. Now, unless she remembers to crawl around on her hands and knees and pull out the wall plug before she goes to bed, she can be reasonably certain of a five-thirty wake-up call. I suggested turning the sound down to zero but have not checked to see if it works. Perhaps the flickering light will wake her, too.

Does the cat understand that it can access sleep-disturbing sound clutter and thereby get fed early by hanging down over the face of a television set and pulling a button with its teeth? Apparently. There is a lot of complex baggage that goes into that series of acts, events, and results, however, and dragging one's feet before answering is allowed. In fact, it is recommended.

ROGER A. CARAS

21

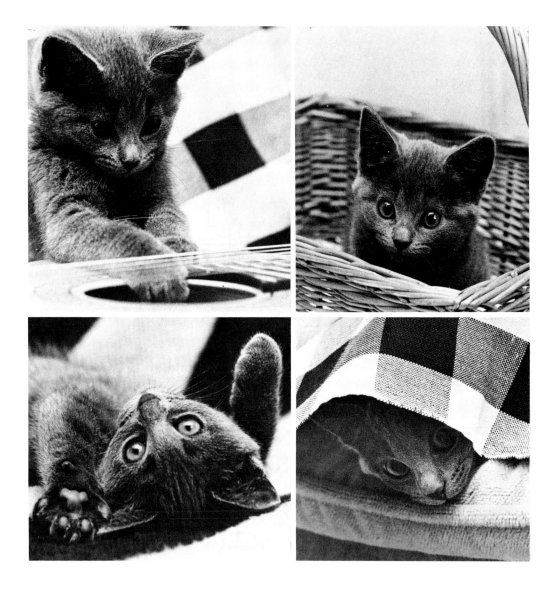

Cat's cradle,
Cat's slumber,
Soft slumber;
Sleep softly
All cats.

Drowsy, drowsy,
Dozing away the futile hours,
What wouldn't you give to be a cat
Instead of what you are?

PAUL GALLICO

Games and recreations, including fireside reading, letter writing, and small household repairs: these categories don't refer to yours but to theirs, and they are not to be tolerated unless you, yourself, have something better to do. Any indulgence by your people in the above must be on sufferance and with your permission. You must establish firmly and quickly, once and for all, that they are not to participate in any of them if you happen to want attention. Under 'games' we consider any such pastimes as scrabble, dominoes, chess, checkers (and in the old days, mah-jongg), card games of any kind, ping-pong, badminton, etc.

Every well-educated house cat ought to know when and how to break them up. For instance, there is no point in interfering with a scrabble game at the very beginning. They will only shoo you away, and if you persist, throw you out or shut you up in another room. Such procedure shows not only lack of instruction but failure to appreciate the psychology of people, which, in a house cat, is a far more serious defect. The proper method is to wait until the board is practically full with a most complicated arrangement of words. *Then*, jump up onto the board with the most sweetly saccharine 'Purrrrrrmaow' that you can muster, scatter the pieces in all directions, sit down, and commence to wash.

They will be absolutely furious with you for a moment, but never forget they are potty over you, or they would never let you get away with everything you do in the house. It will be too much trouble for them to try to remember the words they had formed, or the pattern of the letters. Hence it will be far easier to skip the whole thing and pay attention to you, or go and do something else.

The same goes for dominoes, chess, checkers, parchesi, snakes and ladders, and anything at all with a board and movable pieces. Scatter the pieces. Sit on the board.

Ping-pong, of course, is a setup. The first time the ball hits the floor, fall on it, tackle it, pass it, dribble it, juggle and run with it. They will instantly become far more interested in watching *you* at play than in playing themselves. And, incidentally, this is an excellent and simple way to teach them how much you enjoy a ping-pong ball and get them to supply you with your own, which you will keep amongst your toys.

Card games are more difficult to break up, with the exception of Solitaire, where you are dealing with only one person, who is bored and lonely or he wouldn't be playing Solitaire, which means that you are halfway home. When you see that he has a game nicely laid out, jump up onto the table and sit on the cards. If he attempts to push you away, push back, rubbing up against his hands, arms, or shoulders and purring violently. You will see, he will give up the game because, apparently, your need for companionship is greater than his.

Interfering with a bridge table or a poker session is much more difficult and, actually, not advisable, and no smart house cat will attempt it, though it can be done. It is much easier to prevent two people from having a quiet evening of relaxation and entertainment than to break up an organized card party with a house full of guests. To do so, to stop all activity and centre it upon yourself, you must actually provide more entertainment and novelty than may be had from the cards. In other words, clown it to the extent where you lose dignity and the game is no longer worth the candle.

When you see your person settle down to do some fireside or after-dinner reading, jump up into his or her lap, get comfortable, and then put your paws across the book or paper. This will make turning the pages difficult, and after a while you will find they will give up.

Letter-writing is even easier to break up, since none of them really and truly want to write letters. Here you use a more direct technique, which is to get on the table or desk and lie down on the writing paper. If they persist, begin to make little passes at the pen with your paw, as though it were a game. In the old days, before they all had mechanical pens, we used to upset the ink bottle, which was most effective, even though it sometimes got us into serious trouble, but the lesson of the overturned ink bottle was never forgotten. Still, today if you will continue to play with the pen, eventually the letter writer will say, 'Oh, Kitty, you are a nuisance,' but it will be said, actually, with relief, for it means he can put off writing letters till another day with a clear conscience.

I find I have forgotten to mention another interference, which can be the greatest sport. Many people don't use a pen or a pencil, but instead a machine known as a typewriter, for writing letters or even doing work. If you are so fortunate as to happen to have chosen an author to live with, you may spend the most delightful hours interfering with his effort, for which he will be most grateful to you, since every author I have ever heard of will seize upon the slightest excuse to avoid writing. And, at the same time, you can have a marvellous game yourself.

The principle of the typewriter, you will soon learn, is that as the author presses down a key on the keyboard, a bar bearing a letter rises up from its innards and strikes the paper. *Your* game is to see whether you can be quick enough with your paw to catch the letter before it strikes the paper. It is glorious sport and wonderful exercise, and one of the best things about it is that you can play even when the author is not there, for you can press down the keys yourself with one paw and go for the bar with the other.

PAUL GALLICO

W e can go to cats we don't know, any young cats in fact, and watch play behaviour. Watch a kitten or young cat stalk a bit of fluff, move around it, lay a trap for it, and then pounce for the kill. That cat knows it isn't chasing a mouse. The object of the mock attack is failing to give off all kinds of real mouse signals, and yet the cat is turning the inanimate material into a make-believe mouse, it is using its imagination (whatever that really is in cats). Make-believe or 'pretend', as my granddaughter calls it, takes intelligence, and we often judge the progress of children by how imaginative they are, how inventive. Cats are enormously inventive when it comes to turning each other or all kinds of passive objects and material into enemies and prey. They turn their entire world into one big educational toy.

Two cats rearing and swatting at each other, making mock attacks, are creating in their play a make-believe life situation and are both enjoying themselves and learning from their efforts. And it is good exercise. The fact that the cats in play battles frequently change roles —one the aggressor one minute and the other the next—shows that they are not serious. Play behaviour is a yardstick of intelligence, and the range of imaginary objects and situations used in play an even more refined measurement. Cats rank very high on both scales. The incoming sensory deluge pouring its signals into a cat's brain triggers marching orders in a highly developed, wonderfully sharp, and truly creative organ. Anyone who doubts this probably has not spent much time watching cats.

ROGER A. CARAS

The cat went here and there
And the moon spun round like a top,
And the nearest kin of the moon,
The creeping cat, looked up.
Black Minnaloushe stared at the moon,
For, wander and wail as he would,
The pure cold light in the sky
Troubled his animal blood.
Minnaloushe runs in the grass
Lifting his delicate feet.
Do you dance, Minnaloushe, do you dance?
When two close kindred meet,
What better than call a dance?
Maybe the moon may learn,
Tired of that courtly fashion,
A new dance turn.
Minnaloushe creeps through the grass
From moonlit place to place,
The sacred moon overhead
Has taken a new phase.
Does Minnaloushe know that his pupils
Will pass from change to change,
And that from round to crescent,
From crescent to round they range?
Minnaloushe creeps through the grass
Alone, important and wise,
And lifts to the changing moon
His changing eyes.

W. B. YEATS

I walk on secret feet,
Though if I willed,
My tread
Would shake the earth beneath me.
I stalk
As silently as moonrise,
The sinking of a leaf,
The touch of snow upon the ground.
A drop of dew, born to a petal,
The frost spreading upon a windowpane,
The shadow of a cloud
Drifting,
Make no more sound than I.
Nor with my hunting
Do I stir a fallen leaf.
I come,
I go,
Unheard by day,
Unseen by night,
On muffled feet of steel
Clad in velvet shoes.

PAUL GALLICO

A cat brought from Havana by Mademoiselle Aïta de la Penuela, a young Spanish artist whose studies of white angoras may still be seen gracing the printsellers' windows, produced the daintiest little kitten imaginable. It was just like a swan's-down powder-puff, and on account of its immaculate whiteness it received the name of Pierrot. When it grew big this was lengthened to Don Pierrot de Navarre as being more grandiose and majestic.

Don Pierrot, like all animals which are spoiled and made much of, developed a charming amiability of character. He shared the life of the household with all the pleasure which cats find in the intimacy of the domestic hearth. Seated in his usual place near the fire, he really appeared to understand what was being said, and to take an interest in it.

His eyes followed the speakers, and from time to time he would utter little sounds, as though he too wanted to make remarks and give his opinion on literature, which was our usual topic of conversation. He was very fond of books, and when he found one open on a table, he would lie on it, look at the page attentively, and turn over the leaves with his paw; then he would end by going to sleep, for all the world as if he were reading a fashionable novel.

Directly I took up a pen he would jump on my writing-desk and with deep attention watch the steel nib tracing black spider-legs on the expanse of white paper, and his head would turn each time I began a new line. Sometimes he tried to take part in the work, and would attempt to pull the pen out of my hand, no doubt in order to write himself, for he was an aesthetic cat, like Hoffman's Murr, and I strongly suspect him of having scribbled his memoirs at night on some house-top by the light of his phosphorescent eyes. Unfortunately these lucubrations have been lost.

Don Pierrot never went to bed until I came in. He waited for me inside the door, and as I entered the hall he would rub himself against my legs and arch his back, purring joyfully all the time. Then he proceeded to walk in front of me like a page, and if I had asked him, he would certainly have carried the candle for me. In this fashion he escorted me to my room and waited while I undressed; then he would jump on the bed, put his paws round my neck, rub noses with me, and lick me with his rasping little pink tongue, while giving vent to soft inarticulate cries, which clearly expressed how pleased he was to see me again. Then when his transports of affection had subsided, and the hour for repose had come, he would balance himself on the rail of the bedstead and sleep there like a bird perched on a bough. When I woke in the morning he would come and lie near me until it was time to get up. Twelve o'clock was the hour at which I was supposed to come in. On this subject Pierrot had all the notions of a concierge.

At that time we had instituted little evening gatherings among a few friends, and had formed a small society, which we called the Four Candles Club, the room in which we met being, at it happened, lit by four candles in silver candlesticks, which were placed at the corners of the table.

Sometimes the conversations became so lively that I forgot the time, at the risk of finding, like Cinderella, my carriage turned into a pumpkin and my coachman into a rat.

Pierrot waited for me several times until two o'clock in the morning, but in the end my conduct displeased him, and he went to bed without me. This mute protest against my innocent dissipation touched me so much that ever after I came home regularly at midnight. But it was a long time before Pierrot forgave me. He wanted to be sure that it was not a sham repentance; but when he was convinced of the sincerity of my conversion, he deigned to take me into favour again, and he resumed his nightly post in the entrance-hall.

To gain the friendship of a cat is not an easy thing. It is a philosophic, well-regulated, tranquil animal, a creature of habit and a lover of order and cleanliness. It does not give its affections indiscriminately. It will consent to be your friend if you are worthy of the honour, but it will not be your slave. With all its affection, it preserves its freedom of judgment, and it will not do anything for you which it considers unreasonable; but once it has given its love, what absolute confidence, what fidelity of affection! It will make itself the companion of your hours of work, of loneliness, or of sadness. It will lie the whole evening on your knee, purring and happy in your society, and leaving the company of creatures of its own kind to be with you. In vain the sound of caterwauling reverberates from the house-tops, inviting it to one of those cats' evening parties where essence of red-herring takes the place of tea. It will not be tempted, but continues to keep its vigil with you. If you put it down it climbs up again quickly, with a sort of crooning noise, which is like a gentle reproach. Sometimes, when seated in front of you, it gazes at you with such soft, melting eyes, such a human and caressing look, that you are almost awed, for it seems impossible that reason can be absent from it.

Don Pierrot had a companion of the same race as himself, and no less white. All the imaginable snowy comparisons it were possible to pile up would not suffice to give an idea of that immaculate fur, which would have made ermine look yellow.

I called her Seraphita, in memory of Balzac's Swedenborgian romance. The heroine of that wonderful story, when she climbed the snow peaks of the Falberg with Minna, never shone with a more pure white radiance. Seraphita had a dreamy and pensive character. She would lie motionless on a cushion for hours, not asleep, but with eyes fixed in rapt attention on scenes invisible to ordinary mortals.

Caresses were agreeable to her, but she responded to them with great reserve, and only to those of people whom she favoured with her esteem, which it was not easy to gain. She liked luxury, and it was always in the newest armchair or on the piece of furniture best calculated to show off her swan-like beauty, that she was to be found. Her toilette took an immense time. She would carefully smooth her entire coat every morning, and wash her face with her paw, and every hair on her body shone like new silver when brushed by her pink tongue. If anyone touched her she would immediately efface all traces of the contact, for she could not endure being ruffled. Her elegance and distinction gave one an idea of aristocratic birth, and among her own kind she must have been at least a duchess. She had a passion for scents. She would plunge her nose into bouquets, and nibble a perfumed handkerchief with little paroxysms of delight. She would walk about on the dressing-table sniffing the stoppers of the scent-bottles, and she would have loved to use the violet powder if she had been allowed.

Such was Seraphita, and never was a cat more worthy of a poetic name.

Don Pierrot de Navarre, being a native of Havana, needed a hot-house temperature. This he found indoors, but the house was surrounded by large gardens, divided up by palings through which a cat could easily slip, and planted with big trees in which hosts of birds twittered and sang; and sometimes Pierrot, taking advantage of an open door, would go out hunting of an evening and run over the dewy grass and flowers. He would then have to wait till morning to be let in again, for although he might come mewing under the windows, his appeal did not always wake the sleepers inside.

He had a delicate chest, and one colder night than usual he took a chill which soon developed into consumption. Poor Pierrot, after a year of coughing, became wasted and thin, and his coat, which formerly boasted such a snowy gloss, now put one in mind of the lustreless white of a shroud. His great limpid eyes looked enormous in his attenuated face. His pink nose had grown pale, and he would walk sadly along the sunny wall with slow steps, and watch the yellow autumn leaves whirling up in spirals. He looked as though he were reciting Millevoye's elegy.

There is nothing more touching than a sick animal; it submits to suffering with such gentle, pathetic resignation.

Everything possible was done to try and save Pierrot. He had a very clever doctor who sounded him and felt his pulse. He ordered him asses' milk, which the poor creature drank willingly enough out of his little china saucer. He lay for hours on my knee like the ghost of a sphinx, and I could feel the bones of his spine like the beads of a rosary under my fingers. He tried to respond to my caresses with a feeble purr which was like a death rattle.

When he was dying he lay panting on his side, but with a supreme effort he raised himself and came to me with dilated eyes in which there was a look of intense supplication. This look seemed to say: 'Cannot you save me, you who are a man?' Then he staggered a short way with eyes already glazing, and fell down with such a lamentable cry, so full of despair and anguish, that I was pierced with silent horror.

He was buried at the bottom of the garden under a white rosebush which still marks his grave.

Seraphita died two or three years later of diphtheria, against which no science could prevail.

She rests not far from Pierrot. With her the white dynasty became extinct, but not the family. To this snow-white pair were born three kittens as black as ink.

Let him explain this mystery who can.

THEOPHILE GAUTIER

52

There was an old table tennis table in the far shed, and kitten ping-pong soon became an established sport in the Animal Kingdom, providing us with some of the most enjoyable memories of our lives with the cats. The game in fact resembled piggy-in-the-middle far more than it did table tennis, with the kittens as piggies gathered on both sides of the net, doing all in their power to foil our attempts to get the ball across to each other. The game was thus one of man versus cat, with two players comprising the human team, and as many cats as wished to play making up the feline side. The point of the game, as far as we were concerned, was to keep rallies going as long as possible. Any rally of over four strokes constituted a point in our favour; any over nine gave us the game, this however being purely theoretical, never occurring in reality. Any rally that our opponents put a stop to before it reached five strokes was of course a point to them. The only other rule was that humans would not use their bats to clear the deck of their opponents or otherwise cause them physical injury . . .

Every year would see the emergence of a new star or two whose skill and enthusiasm would set them apart and make some of their team-mates look like real sluggards. Of these stars, the most memorable was Mac, a beautiful little blue tabby. She would leap skywards for the ball when most other kittens just reared up on their hind legs, and she was the only one who succeeded more than just occasionally in catching the ball in mid-flight with both forepaws. Moreover, she never let herself be distracted from the target, unlike many other kittens who would often divert their attention to games of footsy with each other under the net.

JEREMY ANGEL

THE CAT: Grey or Blue

Represents dignity

A noble, individualistic and sophisticated cat, and one who knows it. It is usually intelligent but appears to be a bit snobbish and very busy doing its own thing. The grey cat gives the impression of a cool, calm character, but I feel this can hide a nervousness, and it is happiest in a steady home. Grey has a detached, dignified feeling and the independent air of this cat can make it appear self-assured. Grey cats are not very common and are often sought by people wishing to have a more unusual colour. It can be very affectionate and gentle on its own terms and this gives us the feeling of being honoured by its attention, which indeed we are.

THE CAT OWNER: Grey and Blue

The owner of a grey cat may have a desire to be different: elegant and sophisticated, with an almost regal air. Such people may be careful in choosing friends, making the most of their talents and often putting in a lot of work along one line of activity. This could be the result of a grey cat person being a little detached and consequently concentrating on an activity that absorbs his or her energies. Grey seems to reflect two main characteristics: one is calmness and a laid-back attitude—a cool cat; the other, depression—I'm feeling blue. Either of these feelings could reflect a grey cat owner. Some people may choose a grey cat to calm their otherwise busy and hectic lives, enabling them to be in touch with their own inner calm. Sometimes, if a grey cat owner has a rather bland, indifferent air, he or she will be hiding a slight nervousness and may need time to accept change and make new friends.

VIVIENNE ANGUS

W hen I have things to say
I expect you to listen to me.
If you cannot understand what I am saying
That is your fault and your loss,
But at least be quiet when I am speaking
And try to comprehend
You who think yourselves so clever,
Who know languages of the people
Of the living world and the dead,
Why cannot you learn mine
Which is so simple
To express wants so few?
'In'
'Out'
'Hungry'
'Thirsty'
'Give me just a taste of what you are having.'
'Something hurts.'
'My ball has rolled under the divan; get it out.'
'Stop doing whatever it is you are doing and pay more attention to
    me.'
'I like you.'
'I don't like you.'
If you can talk to the Arabs, the Chinese, the Eskimos
And read the hieroglyphics of the past, why cannot you understand
    me?
Try!

PAUL GALLICO

I have written elsewhere of a black cat called Tom. He didn't belong to us and in fact we never knew where he came from, but he took to hanging around our place, mingling easily with our own cats and our dogs. He took a special fix on our daughter Pamela, who was then a college student. That in itself was not unusual because most animals take to Pamela as if she were St. Francis. Animals that will not go near another human being, feral dogs and cats, obstreperous horses that are homicidal with anyone else, they all home in on Pamela and literally eat out of her hand. And so it was with Tom. He was a perfectly pleasant animal with everyone else, animal or human, but Pamela was at the centre of his universe, at least when she was around. The mystery lay in the fact that he was around only when she was.

Tom would come when Pamela was home for a long weekend or a holiday and then vanish the moment she went back to school. We never found him casing our place or checking us out. Somehow he knew in other ways, and when Pamela was away, so was he.

Now this is where it gets spooky. When Pamela was due home, almost invariably Tom (we called him that for obvious reasons) would be sitting on the front steps or at the end of the driveway waiting as she pulled in in her car. It happened far too often to be coincidence. He never once appeared when Pamela was not due. Somehow the cat, whose actual identity and home we never learned, would know when Pamela was driving the two hundred or so miles from her campus in New Jersey. He would come from wherever he came and be there before she arrived. I am not certain Pamela fully accepted the idea that he was only on hand when she was due, but there are many witnesses to that truth.

We had no other black cats at the time so mistaken identity isn't a possibility. When Tom was there you knew it. He came into the house at mealtime with our own regular feline herd and there is no overlooking a very large, full-faced, jet black tom that curls up on a chair or couch and waits for his one and only true love. At times he never even made it into the house. He cut it so close that it was only minutes before Pamela appeared that Tom would take up his station outside.

It is difficult to ascribe Tom's repeated accomplishment to seeing, hearing, smelling, tasting, or touch. There was nothing to see, hear, smell, taste, or touch when Tom materialised out of nowhere after being absent for weeks or months. Can time run backwards for cats as well as people? Was Tom remembering the good times with Pamela he was going to have when he made his way to our house? Or could he see or hear or smell, taste or touch Pamela getting into her car two hundred miles away and sense the way in which she was driving?

ROGER A. CARAS

Softest, sweetest, most
incomprehensible thing.

WILLIAM KEAN SEYMOUR

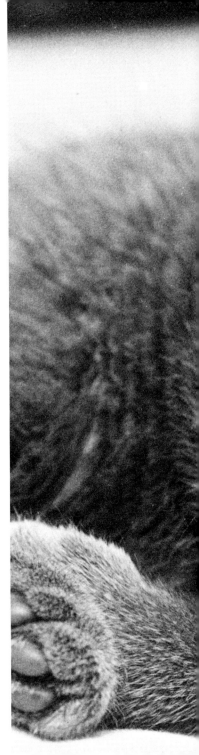

The firelight flickers on the Chinese tray
And on the books set snugly in their rack;
Copper and silver flow beneath its play,
The chairs are placed—what is it that we lack?

She comes. With each foot delicately placed,
Advancing like a vestal to the rite,
She scorns to move with unbecoming haste
Or note the lesser objects in her sight.

She settles couchant; curves one placid paw
Beneath her chest; now curves its mate the same;
Yields to the prompting of some ancient law
And fastens thoughtful eyes upon the flame.

Now let the night wind rise, the grey storm come.
The cat in on the hearth—we are at home.

SILENCE BUCK BELLOWS